ROSLEY

SCHOOL

Other books by Jean Ure

For older readers

HI THERE, SUPERMOUSE!
NICOLA MIMOSA
WHO SAYS ANIMALS DON'T HAVE RIGHTS?
WILLIAM IN LOVE

For teenage readers

SEE YOU THURSDAY

ROSLEY

SCHOOL

The Phantom Knicker Nicker

Jean Ure

Illustrated by
Mark Southgate

PUFFIN BOOKS

For the original Cyril Durkin,
who couldn't eat rhubarb. . .

PUFFIN BOOKS

Published by the Penguin Group
Penguin Books Ltd, 27 Wrights Lane, London W8 5TZ, England
Penguin Books USA Inc., 375 Hudson Street, New York, New York 10014, USA
Penguin Books Australia Ltd, Ringwood, Victoria, Australia
Penguin Books Canada Ltd, 10 Alcorn Avenue, Toronto, Ontario, Canada M4V 3B2
Penguin Books (NZ) Ltd, 182–190 Wairau Road, Auckland 10, New Zealand

Penguin Books Ltd, Registered Offices: Harmondsworth, Middlesex, England

First published by Blackie Children's Books 1993
Published in Puffin Books 1995
3 5 7 9 10 8 6 4 2

Text copyright © Jean Ure, 1993
Illustrations copyright © Mark Southgate, 1993
All rights reserved

The moral right of the author has been asserted

Printed in England by Clays Ltd, St Ives plc
Filmset in 16/20pt Linotype ITC Cheltenham

Chapter One

GANG OF FOUR PRIVATE DETECTIVE AGENCY

Priya printed the words carefully in her best handwriting, in bold black felt-tip pen, on the back of an old piece of card. She looked round at the rest of the Gang – little chubbly Alice, with her baby blue eyes and cherubic face, long skinny Vas and pink plump Toby. They were seated in a row on top of the wall by the bus shelter on the village green, idly swinging their legs in the summer sunshine.

'What else shall I say?'

Alice took hold of one of the stubby blonde plaits which stuck out like little fat sausages on either side of her head. She did her best to pull it round as far as her mouth. (It was Alice's ambition to be able to chew on the end of it.)

'It was your idea,' said Alice. 'You think what to say.'

'I shall say, **Mysteries Solved**,' said Priya. '**For a Fee**.'

Alice attempted to tie both plaits under her chin in a knot.

'How much are we going to charge?'

'Five pounds?' said Priya.

'Ten,' said Vas.

'Ten if it's dangerous.'

Alice squealed. 'I don't want to do anything dangerous!'

'You might have to,' said Priya. 'When you set out to solve mysteries there's no telling where you might end up.'

Alice put a thumb in her mouth and started to suck.

'What I'll do,' said Priya, picking up the card, 'I'll stick it in the window when my dad's not looking.'

Priya's dad ran the Tipsy Green post

office and newsagent's, just across from the bus shelter where they were sitting. They could see the window quite clearly, with all its cards advertising goods for sale, rooms to let, services for hire. People were supposed to pay 50p a week to have their cards in the window, but the Gang didn't have 50p. They didn't have 20p.

They didn't even have 5p. The Gang were broke.

'By this time next week – ' Priya sprang down triumphantly from the wall – 'we'll be rich as rich! And all thanks to me!'

Toby took his specs off and began energetically to polish them. 'That's boasting, that is.'

'Pooh!' said Priya, doing a little showing-off twirl and losing her balance.

Toby hastily put his specs on again as Priya went spinning, out of control, round the corner of the bus shelter. Boing! went Priya, hurtling into someone coming in the opposite direction. A big hand shot out and grabbed her.

'Watch it!' said a familiar voice.

The voice belonged to the Lead Truncheon (otherwise known as Sergeant Durkin of the local nick). The Lead Truncheon was an old enemy.

'What are you lot up to?' he said.

They looked at one another. They could hardly say they were planning to cheat Priya's dad out of 50p. It wasn't the sort of thing you said to a policeman. Alice dimpled prettily.

'We're working out what to do during the holidays,' she said.

'Is that so?' said the Lead Truncheon. He wasn't taken in by Alice's dimples, nor by her cherubic face. People who had never met Alice before automatically assumed that she must be such a nice little, sweet little, good little thing. Miss Pentelow, at school, had once mistakenly cast her as an angel in the nativity play. The Lead Truncheon would never have cast her as an angel: he knew her too well.

'Just you make sure,' growled the Lead Truncheon, 'that you behave yourselves.'

The Lead Truncheon bowled off across the road. In worried tones, Vas said, 'What are we doing that's wrong?'

'Nothing,' said Priya. 'He's just trying to put the frighteners on.'

'Well, he can try all he likes, we're not breaking any of his rotten old laws so ha ha and sucks to him,' said Alice, thumbing her nose at the Lead Truncheon's retreating back.

'It could be said that we are actually

helping,' agreed Priya. 'Imagine if someone came and asked us to catch a real criminal!'

'Like a bank robber,' said Toby.

'Or an international thug,' said Alice.

'And we ran them to earth and cornered them!'

'We could charge simply *oodles*!'

They sat, entranced at the prospect. Alice distinctly saw herself staggering home under the weight of two big money bags. Toby had visions of suitcases full of banknotes. Priya rather fancied appearing on television –

GIRL DETECTIVE CATCHES WORLD NUMBER ONE CROOK . . .

They were brought back to earth, as usual, by Vas. Vas did tend to take life rather seriously.

'Is it very likely, do you think?'

Priya looked at him, haughtily.

'Is what very likely?'

'That anyone would ask us to catch a real criminal.' (Let alone a bank robber or an international thug.)

'Anything is likely,' said Priya, 'once you set up in the private detective business.' She snatched the card off the top of the wall. 'All we've got to do now is just sit back and wait!'

14

Chapter Two

'I'm getting bored,' grumbled Alice. 'Three days it's been in your dad's window, that notice has.'

Three whole days and not a single inquiry . . . three whole days spent sitting on the wall, until their bottoms were sore and the Lead Truncheon was beginning to grow suspicious.

'Just remember,' he said, 'I've got my eyes on you. All four of 'em . . . two at the front and two at the back. There's nothing happens in this place escapes my notice.'

'That's 'cause nothing ever happens,' muttered Alice.

This morning Priya had had one of her bright ideas. 'Cop this!' (Priya's language was a source of great distress to her parents. They didn't think it was quite nice.) 'See what I've done!'

With a flourish, Priya unfurled a large sheet of paper. On the paper, in big letters, it said:

LOCAL CRIMEBUSTERS!
Let us solve your crimes for you
For a Fee

'Oh, wow!' said Alice.
'Brilliant!' breathed Toby.
'I did it last night,' said Priya, trying to sound modest and not succeeding.

'What I thought, we'd stick it on the wall so's everyone can see as they go past.'

'What happens if it rains?' said Vas.

Alice groaned.

Priya said, 'Listen, dummy! How's it going to rain? The sky's blue as can be.'

She handed the sheet of paper to Toby – 'Hold that while I stick it up. Well, hold it *straight*, dummy!' She was just ripping off a length of Sellotape with her teeth when the ground shook beneath their feet and the Lead Truncheon came trundling out from behind the bus shelter.

'You wouldn't be thinking of affixing that nasty horrible poster to that nice bare wall, would you, by any chance? 'Cause if you were you would be breaking the law and I would have to arrest you. You have been warned.'

The Gang watched resentfully as the Lead Truncheon trod across the road to the Tipsy Newsagent's. As he stepped on to the pavement on the opposite side a small spidery figure came scuttling up from behind and

poked him in the back. The Lead Truncheon sprang round as if he had been shot.

'Who did that?'

It was only old Annie. (The Gang always referred to her as old Annie. Priya's dad, more respectfully, referred to her as Mrs Smith.)

'Here, you!' said Annie, prodding the Lead Truncheon with a bony finger. 'I want a word with you.'

'Certainly, madam.' The Lead Truncheon drew himself up. 'How can I be of assistance?'

'What I was wondering,' said Annie, 'was if you could possibly take a few minutes off from busting big crime to come and investigate the mystery of my drawers.'

'Your what?' said the Lead Truncheon.

'My drawers,' said Annie.

'What's happening to your drawers?'

'Someone's nicking 'em, that's what.'

'Nicking your drawers?'

'That is what I said,' said Annie.

'I see.' The Lead Truncheon nodded, intelligently. 'Someone is nicking your drawers . . . a strange thing to nick, if I may say so.'

'I can't stop you,' said Annie. 'It's a free country. Say what you like. All I want is me drawers back.'

'Quite. I appreciate that.' The Lead Truncheon took out his notebook. He opened it and made some marks. 'Very well, then, Annie. I mean, madam. I shall send someone to investigate. Rest assured, we shall stop at nothing to apprehend the criminal and restore the stolen property.'

The Lead Truncheon trod onwards, down the village street. Annie, with a disgruntled sniff, headed for the news-agent's.

'Well!' said Priya. She turned excitedly to the others. 'This could be of interest!'

They watched as Annie and Mr Patel came to the shop doorway. Mr Patel was holding a piece of card.

'I thought I'd give it a go,' said Annie. 'Try advertising in your window. Lovely pair of vases, they are. Genuine from Broadstairs. Thought I might get a bob or two for them.'

'I am sure that you will,' said Mr Patel. He was scanning the window, looking for a space to put the card. Suddenly, he stiffened. 'What is this?' He darted inside, snatched something out of the frame and ran frenziedly back again.

'"Gang of Four Private Detective Agency"? What is this thing doing in my window?'

Discreetly, the Gang of Four melted out of sight behind the bus shelter.

They heard Priya's dad reading out the rest of the card – '"Mysteries solved"? "For a fee"?' His voice rose, shrill with outrage. '"Ask inside for Ms Patel"?' Then they heard old Annie.

'I'd pay a fee quick enough to anyone that could solve the mystery of my disappearing drawers . . . that's three pairs I've had nicked. Wait for that Sergeant Durkin, you could wait for ever. Couldn't catch a knicker nicker if he came on one red-handed!'

Chapter Three

'You heard her!' gloated Priya. 'She'd pay *anyone*.'

'Three pairs!' marvelled Alice. 'That's six drawers! If we could find all six – '

'We could charge £5 a drawer!' Toby polished his specs, excitedly. Now he had visions not just of suitcases full of money but of whole wheelbarrows full. He jammed his specs back on to his nose. 'What are we waiting for? Let's get started!'

It was just a question of finding out where old Annie lived.

'We'll ask my dad,' said Priya. 'He'll know.'

Priya had momentarily forgotten that her dad was mad at her for cheating him out of 50p. It wasn't until she was half-way through the door that she remembered.

'You! Come here! I want a word with you!'

Mr Patel flew at her, from behind the counter. The rest of the Gang hastily retreated. Two seconds later, Priya came catapulting out to join them.

'What happened?' said Alice.

'He wouldn't give it me. We'll have to think of some other way of finding out.' This was where real detective work came in. 'Step number one – '

'It's all right,' said Alice. 'We've already got it.'

Priya's mouth dropped open. 'How?'

'Looked at her card in the window . . . she lives at 4 Rose Cottages.'

'Right!' Priya flipped her plait. (Priya's plait, unlike Alice's two little sausages, was long and thick. It hung half-way down her back.) 'Let's go!'

They set off across the Green, Toby, Alice and Priya in the lead, Vas lagging a bit. Vas had been brooding, turning things over in his mind.

'What's a knicker nicker?' he said.

They turned to look at him.

'Pardon?' said Priya.

'What she said . . . couldn't catch a knicker nicker if he came on one red-handed.'

'She was talking about the Lead Truncheon.'

'I know that,' said Vas.

'So what's the problem?'

'I don't understand – ' Vas said it slowly – 'how a knicker nicker comes into it.'

For all his great brain, Vas did

sometimes have difficulty with things which to other, simpler, people seemed quite obvious.

'See, what it means,' said Alice, kindly, 'it means the Lead Truncheon's so thick that if he came across some- one pinching knickers he wouldn't be able to catch them.'

'But why did she say it?' worried Vas.

'Who knows?' Priya shrugged. In her experience it didn't do to pay too much attention to what grown-ups said. Half the time they denied they'd ever said it, or claimed they'd said something quite different. It was because their brain cells were all starting to decay. 'Let's get a move on before the Lead Truncheon beats us to it!'

Number 4 Rose Cottages was the middle one of a row which clustered behind the churchyard on the far side of the Green. The Gang carefully shut the gate behind them and trod single file up the path. Old Annie appeared at the door.

'Good afternoon, Mrs Smith,' said Priya, politely.

'Afternoon,' said Annie. 'And what can I do for you?'

'We have heard,' said Priya, 'that you are in need of help to catch the person who is making off with your drawers.'

'Never tell me Sergeant Durkin's sent you?' Annie gave a hoarse cackle of laughter. 'I've heard about the police getting younger, but this is ridiculous!'

'We are nothing to do with the police,' said Priya, on her dignity. 'We are the Gang of Four. For a fee we would be willing to assume control of the case.'

'Take four of you, would it?'

'Could be dangerous,' explained Alice. 'Could be an armed gang.'

'What, for my drawers?' Annie gave another of her cackles. 'So what do you want to do? Stake out the premises?'

'That would be our first move,' agreed Priya. 'That is the way we should hope to crack the case.'

'Well, and why not?' Cheerfully, Annie held open the door. 'You couldn't be much more useless than that great lummock of a Durkin. Couldn't catch a knicker nicker if he come on one red-handed!'

Vas plucked urgently at Toby's arm, but Toby, already, was following Alice and Priya into Annie's narrow hallway.

'Might as well get stuck in straight away,' said Annie. She led them down the hall and into a tiny kitchen. 'I've just this minute put them out there . . . one pair of me best drawers.'

She flung open the kitchen door. The Gang peered out.

'Where?' said Priya. She couldn't see

any drawers; only a dustbin, a dilapid-
ated shed, and a washing line full of
washing.

'There!' Annie hobbled out into the
yard. She pointed at a large flapping
garment hanging on the line.

There was a stunned silence; then,
'*Knickers*?' said Priya.

Chapter Four

'That's right,' said Annie. 'Knickers – and someone's nicking 'em! You stay here and keep your eyes peeled. I'm going off upstairs to have a lie down.'

The Gang watched, helplessly, as Annie stomped back into the house and closed the kitchen door behind her.

'*Knickers*,' said Alice, in tones of distaste. She looked at them as they hung there, long and pink and elasticated.

The legs flapped soggily in the breeze. 'I didn't become a private detective to stand guard over a pair of rotten knickers!'

None of them had become private detectives to stand guard over a pair of rotten knickers. Vas opened his mouth to say something, thought better of it and closed it again. Toby put a finger under the bridge of his specs and pushed them half-way up his forehead. It was Priya, as usual, who was the first to regain her fighting spirit.

'If someone's nicking Annie's knickers it's up to us to catch them. Everyone find a hiding place! When I say action stations – '

'What?' said Alice.

'When I say action stations you move!' screamed Priya. 'Action stations!'

Toby dived for cover behind the dustbin, Alice shinned up an apple tree, Priya shot into the shed. Vas, after a moment's hesitation, squeezed himself between a prickly bush and the fence.

There was a silence.

'Now what do we do?' said Alice.

'We wait,' said Priya.

They waited.

'I'm getting bored!' wailed Alice, from out of the branches of her apple tree.

'*Sh*!' hissed Priya.

The waiting went on. And on. And on.

'Bored,' muttered Alice.

CLANG! clattered the dustbin, as Toby lost his balance and went toppling into it.

'What are you doing?' screamed Priya.

'Fell over,' mumbled Toby, groping on the ground for his specs.

'Well, don't!'

'Couldn't help it.'

'Course you could help it! Nobody falls over if they – oo, ow, ouch!'

There was a loud splintering sound as Priya's foot went through the tea-chest she was standing on.

'Bother bother and *blast*!' screeched

Priya. Her dad would have had a fit if he could have heard her.

Vas, reciting football clubs behind his prickly hedge – Arsenal, Bristol City, Crystal Palace, Dundee United – suddenly stiffened as a strange rustling sound came from the other side of the fence. With difficulty, Vas turned himself round. The rustling changed to a snuffling. Could it be the knicker nicker? Knicker nicker with a cold?

Just near by, in the middle of the fence, was a knot-hole. Vas shuffled over to it and applied his eye.

'Yeeeeeurghghgh!' shrieked Vas, rocketing backwards into the prickles.

Priya shot out of her shed, Alice shot out of her tree. Toby fell over again, into the dustbin.

'What happened?' cried Priya.

'It got me!' Vas clambered painfully out of his prickly bush. 'It got me in the eye!'

'What did?' said Alice.

'Was it the knicker nicker?' Toby shunted his specs up his nose and peered fearfully round, as if expecting a fierce knicker nicker to leap the fence at any moment.

'It was . . . *that*!' Vas pointed, dramatically, at the fence. Over the top hung a pair of big doggy paws and a big doggy head, grinning, with half a yard of tongue hanging out. It was the tongue that had done all the damage. 'It's not funny!' shouted Vas.

The dog obviously thought it was; so did Alice. Alice chortled merrily.

'All right! That's quite enough,' said Priya. 'Everyone back to their posts!'

Reluctantly, Alice clambered back up her tree, Toby crouched down behind his dustbin, Vas crammed himself back into his bush. Priya went into her shed and found a flower-pot to stand on.

The dog disappeared. They heard it for a while, groffling about on its own side of the fence, and then there was silence.

Nothing could be heard in Annie's back garden save the sound of bees and the twittering of birds. And then –

'I'm not staying after tea-time,' said Alice, loudly.

'Quiet!' snapped Priya.

Alice subsided, muttering. A few seconds later –

'Oh, look at that lovely butterfly!' said Alice.

A brightly coloured butterfly was skimming to and fro among the flowers.

'Beeeeeeeeeauuuuuuuutiful,' crooned Alice, leaning dangerously out of her branches.

'Get back in that tree!' snapped Priya.

'I want to look at the butterfly!'

'Well, you can't look at the butterfly, we're in hiding.'

'But it's so beeeeeeeeeeeea-uuuuuuuuuutiful,' yodelled Alice, reaching out a hand.

The butterfly, taking fright at the sight of five plump wriggling worms waving at it from an apple tree, rose up out of the flower-bed and went flickering off round the garden. Priya made an angry clicking noise with her tongue. Some people just weren't cut out to be private detectives. The way Alice was carrying on, flapping about in the apple tree like a distracted duck, she'd terrify every criminal for miles around. Who was going to come knicker nicking in a garden where stray arms and legs kept popping out of apple trees?

The butterfly, having completed a couple of laps of Annie's garden, zoomed in on the washing line. It hovered for a while above a nightdress, flitted down a row of stockings, and finally took a fancy to the knickers. The nightdress was a dirty sludge colour, the stockings a boring brown. The knickers, being pink, obviously appealed. The butterfly settled on them, happily.

'Oh!' squeaked Alice, entranced. 'It must think they're a flower!'

Alice began eagerly to descend the tree.

'*Get back!*' hissed Priya.

'But I w—'

'I said, *get back!*'

Alice did so – just in time. A figure was creeping along the lane at the bottom of the garden. It was a man! They could see the top of his head above the fence, and now and again caught glimpses of the rest of him where bits of the fence were missing. The man was bent almost double, stalking stealthily on tiptoe.

At Annie's gate he stopped, rose to his full height and peered in. He had a bald head and a black beard and over his shoulder he carried a canvas bag.

Priya froze on her flower-pot. Alice, in her tree, gripped tightly with both hands. Vas sat on a prickle and didn't even notice. Toby blinked furiously behind his specs.

The Beard leaned forward, over the back gate. He quartered the garden with sinister glare. He didn't notice Alice in her apple tree. His gaze fell greedily upon the knickers. His eyes narrowed. He cast a quick glance up at the house, checking for signs of movement, then back over his shoulder, down the lane.

His hand reached out, fumbling over the top of the gate for the latch. He was coming in!

Chapter Five

Priya, in her potting shed, squinting with one eye through a small square of glass, could just make out the top half of a man's body creeping up the garden. Toby, crouched behind his dustbin, saw a pair of feet coming along the path. Vas, in his bush, saw a pair of knees. It was Alice, in her apple tree, who had the best view.

Alice saw everything. She saw the man peer furtively round the garden as if expecting someone to jump out on him. She saw him close the gate, quietly, quietly, lest anyone should hear. She saw him move on tippity toe, slowly, silently, towards the washing line. She saw his eyes gleam as they fixed upon the knickers. She saw him open the flap of his canvas bag – gently, gently, not to make a sound – and slide something from it. She saw his hand reach out –

At which point, unfortunately, a branch gave way and Alice toppled screaming to the ground.

'Aaaaaaaaaaaaaaaaaaaaaargh!' went Alice, as she landed on a bed of roses.

Needless to say, by the time she had clambered out of it the man had fled.

'After him!' screeched Priya.

They turned, and went racing down the path to the back gate.

'What do we do if we get him?' panted Toby, as they tumbled out into the lane.

'Bash him on the boko!' cried Alice. Alice was rather given to violence. She had once had a fight with a boy at school and knocked two of his teeth out.

'Pulverize him! Spifflicate him! Tear his gizzards out!'

Alice cantered off, bloodthirsty and shrieking, down the lane. Priya streaked after her. Toby followed.

'Wait for me!' yelled Vas, lagging behind as usual.

At the corner, Alice came to a sudden stop. Priya went bundling into her. Toby went bundling into Priya. Vas went bundling into Toby. Alice picked herself up and rubbed crossly at her elbow.

'Do you mind?' said Alice.

'Do you mind?' said Priya.

'Do you mind?' said Toby.

'Always in such a *rush*,' grumbled Alice, who never herself went anywhere at a walk if she could go there at the gallop. 'We don't want him seeing us.'

'That's right!' Priya nodded reprovingly at Vas. 'The idea is to shadow him.'

Single file, with Priya in the lead, the Gang slunk round the corner. Their prey was walking briskly up Tipsy Hill, his canvas bag still slung over a shoulder. He obviously had no idea he was being followed: he was doing his best to look like an ordinary, innocent citizen. No one would have guessed that only a few minutes ago he had been creeping up Annie's garden path hoping to steal her knickers.

Priya scuttled crabwise across the road, heading for the nearest lamp-post. There for a few seconds she

crouched, before breaking cover and racing for shelter behind a parked car. She watched, frowning, as Alice and Toby, like a couple of demented toads, came hopping and scampering in her wake. What *did* they think they were doing? And where was Vas?

Vas was down on his hands and knees, crawling. The trouble with Vas was that he didn't watch television. He didn't watch the police series: he didn't know how it was done. You didn't *crawl*, you *stalked*.

Priya crept stealthily forward, along the side of the parked car. Their man was almost at the top of the hill by now. Another second and he would be out of sight.

That was it! He had gone! Priya broke into a run, reaching the top of

the hill just seconds ahead of Alice.
(Alice might be small, but she could
run fast – and she never liked to miss
out on anything.)

'Where's he gone?' panted Alice.

'Car park, I should think.' He prob-
ably had an accomplice waiting there
with the engine running. Any second

now and they would come roaring past. 'Watch and get his number as he comes out!'

They watched and they watched but the man never came. Where could he be? Where could he have gone?

There was only one place apart from the car park and that was the Tavern itself. But surely a man on the run wouldn't stop off to have a drink?

Or would he?

'It's the only place,' said Toby.

'Unless he knows we're after him and he's hiding in his car till we've given up.'

'Search all the cars!' cried Alice.

There were only five cars in the car park and they were all empty.

Alice said, 'Perhaps he's hiding in a boot,' and Priya, greatly daring, tried all the boots, one after another, and was caught in the act by a woman coming out of the Tavern.

'What are you children doing,' she shouted, 'tampering with my car?'

'We were just checking it for you,' said Priya.

'Checking it was locked,' said Toby.

'And that there wasn't a body in the boot,' added Alice.

'Well, don't!' snapped the woman. 'Otherwise I shall be forced to call the police.'

The woman got into her car and drove off.

'Some people,' said Alice, 'are just so ungrateful.'

'Yes, and some people,' said Priya, 'have really stupid ideas . . . hiding in the boot!'

'He could have been.'

'Well, he wasn't. We'll just have to go and look in the Tavern.'

The Tipsy Tavern was an old building all covered in ivy. On the ground floor there were four long windows with wide, deep windowsills. The Gang crept up to them.

'Take a window each,' hissed Priya, out of the side of her mouth. 'Wait till I give the word . . . I shall count up to three. One – two – three – *go!*'

Four pairs of hands grabbed at the ivy. Four feet planted themselves against the wall. Four bodies hauled themselves up and four pairs of eyes peered in at the windows.

What a shock! Alice nearly fell off her perch for the second time that day. There in front of her was the knicker

nicker, sitting at a table as calm as you like, drinking something out of a big glass mug.

'Cool,' said Priya. 'Very cool.'

They were obviously dealing with a hardened criminal. Any small-time crook would have run off in a panic.

'What do we do now?' Vas wanted to know.

'Surround him,' said Priya.

'On all sides,' urged Alice.

Toby took off his specs and began industriously to polish them.

'You don't think one of us had better go and fetch the Lead Truncheon, do you?'

'In case, you know, he might be dangerous,' said Vas.

'Quick thinking!' said Priya. 'One of us can go and three of us can stay and surround him.'

'I'll go,' said Vas and Toby.

'Alice can go,' said Priya. 'She runs the fastest. Don't forget,' she said to Alice, 'tell him how we practically caught him red-handed. Say we've got him cornered and he's got to come at once and make an arrest. And *be quick*.'

Alice rushed back off down the hill, plaits a-bobbing, cheeks puffed out with the importance of her mission. The rest of the Gang stayed behind to surround the Tavern.

'He's still in there,' hissed Priya, as Alice came panting back up the hill a

few minutes later, followed by the perspiring bulk of the Lead Truncheon.

'Right.' The Lead Truncheon tugged at his cuffs. 'This had better not be a joke or someone will feel the full weight of my tongue. You wait here. I'm going in.'

The Gang stood watching as the Lead Truncheon scrunched off across the gravel.

'What a long time it takes to arrest someone,' sighed Alice, after they had stood there for at least a minute. 'Shall I go and look through the window and see what's happening?'

'No,' said Priya.

'I think I will,' said Alice. 'I'd like to see someone being arrested.'

A moment or so later Alice came back to report that 'All he's doing is just talking.'

'They have to talk,' said Priya, 'before they can put the handcuffs on. They have to say, "We warn you that anything you say may be taken down and used in evidence against you." Then they can arrest you.'

'Oh,' said Alice. She didn't sound very convinced. 'Looked to me,' she said, 'as if they were having a conversation.'

'They do,' said Priya. 'That's what they do. Just wait a minute and you'll see.'

They waited a minute and the Lead Truncheon appeared. By himself. He did not look happy. His face was all mean and crinkled like a bad-tempered turnip.

'Didn't you arrest him?' said Alice.

'Arrest him?' roared the Lead Truncheon. 'Arrest him for what? I'll arrest you if you're not careful! I'll have you up for time-wasting, I'll have you up for mickey-taking, I'll have you up for every crime in the book! The Lead Truncheon's voice rose to a howl of fury. 'You have made me look a right banana! That knicker nicker you so nearly caught red-handed is only a world-famous expert on butterflies!'

There was a silence.

'Butterflies?' said Priya.

'Yes!' snarled the Lead Truncheon. 'Butterflies! He was in the act of trying to photograph some rare species hitherto unknown in this part of the world when a pack of idiotic interfering children fell out of a tree and frightened it away! Next time you decide to finger someone, just make sure he's not a world-famous expert, will you? I do not appreciate,' said the Lead Truncheon, 'being made a laughing stock of!'

Chapter Six

The Gang trailed back, hump-shouldered and dejected, down Tipsy Hill. Everyone was inclined to be rather grumpy, especially with Alice.

'Falling out of a tree!'

'I couldn't help it,' said Alice.

'Of course you could!'

'I jolly well couldn't!'

'You jolly well – '

'It's starting to rain.' Vas made the announcement in tones of gloomy satisfaction. 'I told you it would. The knickers'll be getting wet – if they're still there.'

'Oh!' Alice clapped a hand to her mouth. The knickers! They had forgotten all about them!

'Quick!' Priya set off along the lane at a fast trot. The knicker nicker might be there right now, doing his nicking!

The knicker nicker wasn't there, but the knickers, fortunately, were. They hung damply from the line, all limp and soggy from being rained on.

'Right,' said Priya. 'Let's start again.'

This time, because of the rain, they all crammed together into the shed.

'I'm not staying longer than half-past four,' said Alice. 'The Odd Bods is on.'

'Odd Bods is for children,' said Priya, squashingly.

'I am a child,' said Alice. (It was very difficult to squash Alice. She was one of those people who are virtually un-squashable.)

Priya stood on her flower-pot, and Alice got a flower-pot of her own. They craned to see out of the small square of window. Vas and Toby huddled to-gether by the door.

'Half an hour,' said Alice. 'If nothing's happened by then – '

Even as she spoke, a spine-chilling sound came from outside the shed. It was the sound of heavy breathing. Someone was out there! Someone was prowling about!

'Shut the door!' hissed Priya.

Too late! A horrible hairy arm was already snaking its way through the crack . . .

Alice yelped and fell off her flower-pot. Toby screeched and jumped backwards into Vas. Priya stood staring, rooted to the spot.

The next second, the door crashed open and a big brown shape came bursting in. This time even Priya screamed.

After bouncing three times round the shed, scattering flower-pots in all directions, treading on a garden spade and catching its feet in a bag full of pegs, the shape skidded to a halt. It sat back on its haunches, its tongue lolling pinkly out of the side of its mouth. Its ears pricked forward. It regarded the Gang with bright eyes. What to do next?

Priya wobbled frantically on the rim of her flower-pot. Vas and Toby edged their way through the door. (Ready, as Vas earnestly explained later, to run for help.) Only Alice stayed where she was, rubbing at her ankle which had come into contact with something sharp when she had fallen off her flower-pot.

The shape barked, impatiently.

'Oh, be quiet!' said Alice. 'I've gone and hurt my ankle, thanks to you.'

Taking this as a sign of encouragement, the shape promptly flew at her and began to cover her in passionate wet kisses. Alice pushed at it.

'Gerroff!' said Alice. She scrambled to her feet and pointed, sternly. 'Go!'

With a final loving slurp it went, dragging the peg basket with it. Vas wiped a hand across his brow.

'That was the one that got me,' he said. 'Of course I wasn't scared. I knew it was only a dog.'

'So did I,' said Toby. 'I knew it was only a dog.'

'Funny,' said Priya. 'The way you were carrying on you'd have thought it was a sabre-toothed tiger.'

'It's a boxer,' said Alice. 'There's one lives down our road.'

She clambered on to the broken packing case and pressed her nose back to the window. A loud wail came from her. Priya wobbled again.

'Do you have to?' said Priya.

Alice turned, pop-eyed.

'Help!' shrieked Alice. 'The knickers have gone!'

Chapter Seven

Alice was right: where the knickers had been there was now an empty space.

'But who can have taken them?' wailed Priya. 'They were there a second ago!'

'They're not there now,' said Alice.

Vas, seeing all their efforts go for nothing, gave a howl of rage and tore out of the shed. The others streamed after him. In the middle of the garden, Vas came to a halt.

'*Look*!'

Vas's voice rose quivering with indignation. There, in the act of digging a hole beneath the rose bushes, was their friend with the horrible hairy arm. One leg of Annie's drawers was clamped in its teeth, the other trailing behind it across the mud.

'Stop him!' screeched Toby.

Across the lawn and into the flower-bed they plunged, Alice in the lead.

'You gimme that back!' panted Alice, snatching at the spare knicker leg.

Alice tugged one way, the dog tugged the other. Something was going to have to give; and if it wasn't Alice, and it wasn't the dog –

Rip! went the knickers, parting company right down the middle. Alice and the dog both sat down, very suddenly, on their bottoms.

There was a silence.

'Well, at least we found the thief,' said Toby.

All they had to do now was go and tell Annie.

'She ought to be pretty pleased with us,' said Alice, dangling a small length of mangled knicker leg.

'Pleased?' sniffed Annie, when they had knocked at the kitchen door and she had come downstairs to let them in. 'What have I got to be pleased about? That was a good pair of drawers, that was! Look at 'em now! Only fit for cleaning floors with.'

'If you dug up your flower-bed,' said Toby, trying to be helpful, 'you might find all the other pairs.'

'Oh, might I?' Annie folded her arms. 'And what state do you think they'd be likely to be in?'

The Gang looked at her mutinously. Alice stuck out her lower lip. Toby took his specs off.

'We caught the thief,' muttered Vas.

'Yes, and ruined a pair of me best drawers in the process! I – '

Annie broke off as a great thundering and hammering came from the direction of the front door.

'Here!' said Annie. 'What's going on?'

'Shall I go and have a look?' said Priya.

'I'd better come with you,' said Vas.

'So had I,' said Toby.

'Bother!' said Alice. It was nearly half-past four and Alice wanted to go home and watch the Odd Bods.

Priya and the others came back to report.

'It's the Lead Tr— I mean, Sergeant Durkin,' said Priya. 'I think he wants to come in.'

'Wants to come in? I'll give him wants to come in! He'll be paying for a new door if he's not careful.'

Annie marched off indignantly down the passage. She returned with the Lead Truncheon clumping behind. He sounded like an army on the march.

'I am here,' said the Lead Truncheon, 'to investigate the case of your disappearing – ' he cleared his throat – 'drawers, I believe you said it was?'

'You're too late,' said Annie. 'They've already done it.'

'Oh?' The Lead Truncheon's neck shot out of his collar. His eyes bulged as he looked at the Gang.

'They've found out who's been nicking 'em, they've found out where he's stashed 'em . . . all I need you to do,' said Annie, 'is go and dig up me flower-bed for me.'

'Dig up your flower-bed?' said the Lead Truncheon.

'Recover the stolen property. That's what the police is for, isn't it? Recovering folks' property?'

'That and arresting criminals.' The Lead Truncheon scowled hideously at the Gang. 'That is, when they *are* criminals.'

'This one's a criminal all right,' said Annie. 'Lives right next door to me an' all.'

The Lead Truncheon perked up. He whipped out his notebook.

'Which number?'

'Number 3,' said Annie.

'Number 3 Rose Cottages . . . what's his name?'

'Bonzo,' said Annie.

'Bonzo?'

'Yes, and he's a big ugly brute with a squashed-in face. It'll take at least three of you. But I'll thank you,' said Annie, 'to recover my stolen property for me first, before it comes on to rain again. You'll find a spade in the garden shed.'

With a final glare at the Gang, the Lead Truncheon threw open the kitchen door.

'Don't think I've forgotten,' he said. 'I have a memory like an elephant's. Be warned!'

The door closed as the Lead Truncheon went off to dig in the flower-bed for three pairs of knickers.

'Right,' said Annie, in businesslike tones. 'Let's see.' She picked up her handbag from the kitchen table and took out her purse. 'How much would you say it was worth?'

'Ten pounds?' said Vas.

'On your bike!' said Annie.

'Seven?' said Vas.

'Four,' said Annie.

'Six,' said Vas.

'Five,' said Annie.

'Done!' said Vas.

'That,' said Priya, as they walked back up the lane clutching their hard-earned money, 'is what I call a good day's work!'